MONSTERS

J. Dill

Copyright © 2024 J. Dill
All rights reserved
First Edition

PAGE PUBLISHING
Conneaut Lake, PA

First originally published by Page Publishing 2024

ISBN 979-8-89157-343-7 (pbk)
ISBN 979-8-89157-357-4 (digital)

Printed in the United States of America

Dedicated to all the shutter speeds of anxious minds.

I'm going to count to four. Fours are how I am learning to breathe. Follow my fours. I'll separate with the numbers each time I need to take a breath. The fours will start over again, as they always need to. One, two, three, four…

1

Monsters are real. I won't be ashamed anymore about running from them. If I am afraid, then there is something to fear.

Pound was the first. "Pound, pound, pound!" He was abrasive against my door and inside my chest. He created Pain.

Pain always followed, then I feared her too. Pain came in aches mostly, but occasionally, she was sharp. Sharp was the fiercest form of Pain that I hated the most. She stabbed, pinched, prodded, and sliced. Sharp means clever too. Her cleverness is why she smiled, often appearing as a friend.

After all, monsters are clever. That's why they have existed eternally. They are around long enough that we learn to be afraid, yet they choose to hide at the perfect moments. Their choices make us think we're just crazy and prone to panicking, desperately trying to convince ourselves that "the danger isn't real." Pain can be pacified if you give her enough attention. She'll whisper gently into your ear, "You are healed." Healed, that is, until Pound comes knocking again.

And that's where most people get caught up in the wrong idea. "Wounds heal." Maybe but scars don't. Scars remain, and they can be ripped open. Calloused tissue and a fresh wound all spun together in a web of panic. I was reminded that monsters have no qualms about ripping scars open. In broad daylight. Under the sun.

2

Pound returns often. He returns everywhere. I saw him near the register and started to shake. He didn't want to scare me. Not at first. At first, he wanted me to believe he was apologizing. But I've spent enough time around Pound to know what a fake apology sounds like, "I felt bad about how things went down between us." He couldn't meet my eyes as he spoke. The beady blades of his pupils darted around the room instead. Pound is anxious; his anxiety is part of the reason why he knocks so loudly. Pound sat down, maybe to appear less menacing or maybe because Pound often isn't strong enough to stand. Not on his own. Not without pounding. Not without me.

I was frozen, holding my fizzy Diet Coke… Time slowed and I could hear the tiny bubbles *"pop"* as I looked into Pound's eyes. Empty. Cold. I filled the space between us with random, desperate words, hoping he wouldn't ask about her. "Wow, you work on this side of town, huh? How long have you apprenticed? Apprenticeship sounds so fantastic and formal…"

But that's when Pound reminded me who he was.

He shook his head and spoke in a low, intimidating voice, "I was going to try to find you. I was going to show up at your parents' house because I didn't know where else to go. I didn't know what else to do."

Pound was pretending that he was a victim. He was pretending that he had been lost. But Pound knew exactly where he was the whole time I ran with his daughter. He was inside himself, pacifying himself. He didn't actually care about his daughter. He just wanted to chase us. I looked at Pound's cold eyes now as they pierced me again.

Protective instincts kicked in as he asked for my number. I recited the digits, believing that somehow giving him personal information returned control to me.

If I give him my number, he won't try to find me. He won't pop up unexpectedly again. Pacify him. I shook ever so slightly at the thought of his face appearing out of the air again, but I had to hide my fear from Pound.

Of course I knew then that I would never tell her I ran into him. Pound was a monster. In his own way, he had haunted my daughter's nightmares and her body with the disease he passed onto her, but I wasn't going to let him change his face in front of her. My worst moments with Pound flashed before my eyes as I tried to figure out how to escape him.

He's still real. He has my number. I hoped he had forgotten us, but he remembered and threatened to return. My mind raced as I recalled a past packed with Pound.

His eyes were blue and bloodshot. He smelled of whiskey.

The dark-honey-colored liquor spat through his words and bled out of his pores as he hissed at me, "Maybe you're an alcoholic, not me. Did you ever consider that!"

Pound made me feel strangely, and my veins were suddenly on fire. Adrenaline burned through my arms as I watched Pound's blood pop through the vessels in his nose, tiny rivulets of fury.

"Pound, I just wanted to tell you that you might've had too many. You can't control your balance, and you're hurting. Something in you wants to hurt me. I don't like it."

"No, it's just you, and shut up about my brother too! We don't need you to tell us how to live. Matter of fact, you can take this key and get the fuck out of here and go home if you ever disrespect my family again!" His rising voice was meant to sting. The rage in his eyes was created to crush as he spewed.

What did Pound mean? I questioned.

I believed I was his family. I held his child in my body. My veins were on fire. Pain was being born too. Pound hurt me too badly.

And I couldn't understand. *How could he say this to me? Why was he asking me if I am an alcoholic? Am I? I used to have a few drinks too.*

The liquor blurred Pound in my brain. In the fuzzy, he seemed fun. Oh god. Am I an alcoholic? Wait, he's still staring. I have to think of something to say. But what? I am in danger. I don't understand Pound's eyes or his words. I am in danger. I have to protect her too. I have to avoid Pain. My child. His child. Our child. Why won't Pound take care of me? Doesn't he care about her? Doesn't he know how the fire is burning through my veins, making my heart race and stressing her out too?! What can I do? My mind created. There was lightning in my brain and in my blood, wiring my instincts to speak the language of monsters. Fire.

Pound threw the key at me; the cold metal scratched my face. I felt every millimeter across my hot skin. The cold key opened a stark awareness of Pound.

He won't save me, I thought. *He won't protect her. The danger I feel with him reminds me that I am alive, and I can't leave him. I can't leave him because I don't know if I'm wrong. The red in Pound's eyes and his words felt wrong. He made me feel ashamed, though I don't know what I am ashamed of.* I was ashamed of something that did not exist.

And so Pound helped me create a doubt that slowly morphed into certainty that there was something wrong with me. *He wouldn't be so angry at me if I hadn't done something wrong.* The fire in my blood turned to thick, gelatinous shame in my gut, Pain's favorite place to sting when she appeared.

I continued to stare at Pound as my mind raced. We had created something together, and I was afraid. What would you call what Pound and I created? His fury plus amber whiskey plus my confusion plus fear plus shame plus my protective instincts for myself and my child equals...what?

I don't know. I held something in my brain and blood that Pound gave me, but I couldn't name it. Fear simply became how I lived as I learned the language of monsters, a tongue of defensive, instinctive reactions. I believed that living near Pound, in fear, made me powerful. And since Pain was born next and became my best friend, well then, I had a community. As I pulled my mind back to the present, I remembered that I had to stay connected to Pound, keep a piece of myself there with him so that, at the very least, I could try to keep him at bay. I ignored my other instinct at the time. Hope. I gave Pound my number for her too, hoping he could become more than a monster.

I ignored hope because I knew better.

I watched Pound walk away under the bright sun. I learned in that moment that he would never really be gone. I spent years running from him, but he had always been out there. Night or day, he could appear again. My scar was ripped open. Pound was beating in my chest as I watched him walk away. I would remember him in my skin now as the fire burned through my veins again. I would always look back over my shoulder. I knew I had to expect him to appear, so I did at all times. One can't find herself caught unawares with Pound. If you do, he will eat you alive. I blocked his number the moment he texted me. I shut him out but made sure to search for all manner in which he could find his way in and tried to block them too. I realized then that I had given Pound my number in a moment of panic. Incoherent fight or flight. Perceived control was a form of fighting, or maybe a different kind of flight. Regardless, I wanted nothing to do with him. There was no hope that this Pound would ever become more than a monster. He would exist in my protective instincts alone.

3

At this point, you're probably thinking that Pound sounds aggressive, cruel, and frightening. He is. But he's also loud, and he can smile like Pain. Loud can sound exciting and inclusive when one feels trapped in silence. Evil smiles can look charming when one is lonely. Plus, Pound has a manner of slowly increasing his volume. You don't know what hit you until the day he starts screaming. When he first knocks, it's inviting. Someone's there. If you're afraid, you were in a vulnerable position first, a place where you felt safe. I believed Pound saved me from Him. He left me alone and ashamed when I thought He would always be there. I ran away and found Pound. I didn't know it then, but when I found Pound, he whispered to Pain that she should hold my hand when he left me. Then I would know that Pain should be there whenever Pound walked away. I believed I was safe when I met them.

I opened a mysterious door, and Pound and Pain posed on the other side, smiling together. They said they would protect me. Sometimes I remember Pound fondly, though now he mostly screams in my chest.

The screaming aloud is only at night.

This story is about shame too. I need you to know that in case it's not clear yet. He made me feel ashamed.

Pain and Pound weren't the first friends I made. I tried finding Him in the beginning. That's when I began to wonder if I was wrong, if I was *made* wrong. I spent much of my life following His rules, so I could be right. He taught me that inherently, I was a sinner and following Him would free me. "A sinner." What the fuck is a "sinner"? I was human. I was a creator. I was beautiful, resilient, and adaptive. I needed help, as all humans do, to simply be human and exist in a world that requires cruel instincts to survive. But help wasn't a bad thing. He made me believe that it was. Asking for help meant admitting that I should be ashamed that I couldn't exist as a complete being on my own or alongside my kind. He, a "father," called me to whisper my hopes to him. I did. I still felt ashamed. I still felt like a "sinner." Like a monster. Though the definition of sinner still escaped me. The only thing I understood about sinner was that the word was born from shame.

Soon, I realized I couldn't please Him. The narrative He spoke to me was always the same, "You're a sinner. You should be ashamed."

When you are taught that you are born flawed, born broken, born bleeding, born incomplete, born evil…the only pure, right, and good thing about you is the He that exists inside you… Well then, of course, a shameful life is what you are going to weave. I was told I am shame, so I created a life that would ensure I always felt that way. Ashamed. Sheltered from the power I had to create anything else.

So naturally, it follows that I believed Pound when he told me he could help me escape. When Pound first knocked, he was warm.

His voice was seductive. "Hi. I see you."

Wait, did I forget? Sometimes, Pound has eyes too.

He has eyes when he's not screaming. He saw me when he wasn't screaming.

Just knocking.

I invited him in. He saw me. My heart pounded. I liked Pound's eyes, though something was wrong with them that I couldn't name. There was a wildness in the blue that felt like freedom. Pound was friendly and protective too. Pound helped me see what I wanted. Freedom. I didn't see it then, but Pound was a prisoner of his own freedom. I was afraid of him, but the fear felt inviting. I knew he was a monster. But when I met Pound, I realized I liked monsters.

Sometimes, I liked monsters.

I liked them for a while.

I liked him for a while.

So Pound entered, and I gave him my attention. He began to speak more. The beauty of Pound is that he quickly revealed himself as a monster. He didn't hide until I noticed he could scream.

"I won't go out at night. I am afraid of what I might do," Pound whispered.

"What do you mean?"

"Me? Unfiltered?" Pound said. "I am a scary motherfucker. These thoughts that enter my head… I can't go unchecked."

I didn't want to ask Pound about his thoughts. There was a certainty in his tone as he spoke that terrified me. I didn't want to know more, so I didn't ask. I heard and ignored a voice inside me that said, *Pound's words aren't right. There is something dangerous here and you need to run.* But I didn't want to run. That danger felt wild. There was something inviting about his honesty.

I didn't want to know what Pound thought he might do. But I knew he wasn't lying.

Monsters don't lie.

I don't think they can. In all their evil, they don't lie.

Just pretend.

Pound pretended to feel furious at me a lot. I began to notice a pattern. He screamed and threatened when he felt inadequate inside himself. He was a creator because of the questions he inspired me to ask myself. Questions that He had already instilled in me. Questions that confirmed that I was the broken one, needing fixing. I couldn't be right when I challenged Pound to stop being a monster.

"You made me this way! You make me crazy! You did this!" Pound screamed.

Pound didn't act like a monster with others. I often wondered why his monstrous side emerged only when he was with me. He came in so many forms. Pound was committed to me, and he threatened to leave. Sometimes, Pound followed through on the threat and actually ran away. But he always came back. He was drawn to something in me, and he hated me at the same time. Maybe he didn't hate me, but I felt like he did. Every time Pound returned throughout the years, he wore a different face but had the same eyes. He made the same "pounding" sound. Pound created the perfect space in me for Pain to move in when I tried to hide from him for a little while. Scary and steady. Inconsistently loyal. Consistently a monster.

1

Pound is a lover. Pain is a friend. She's a companion. She comforts me after I've been in danger and makes the shadows feel safe. Pain is with me in the shadows, where I can hide from Pound. When I hid with Pain, I wasn't trying to escape Pound. I only wanted shelter from him for a while.

I found passion with Pain and Pound. Passion is what makes them scary. Everything in me feels alive when I am afraid, not dead and useless as He made me believe. Every sense is alert. Pound is loud and heavy. He reminds me that my body is powerful. My instincts answer only to him. Pain whispers to me what I can endure. I love how she whispers. Passion is interwoven with power and whispers. Both set my heart on edge.

Monsters are real. My mind wants them to be. Their existence means I'm not crazy.

2

BREATHING STILL

Anyway, I think I need to try to explain the monsters' faces more clearly. Though their faces change, I can always recognize them. I know Pain's face better; after all, she's my best friend. She is beautiful. Her pale but warm skin glows when she smiles. Pain's hair covers her eyes, so I don't know their color, but the strands of her hair are long and blond like the sun, nearly blindingly white. Bright. The kind of white that shines with gold. I have always liked watching the light bounce off her hair as she holds my hand. We walked home together every day when I first heard Pound's screams. Pain made the loneliness that followed Pound's aggression seem friendly. I didn't miss Pound anymore when I was with her. She helped me feel strong in his absence. Pain showed me that I didn't need Pound to feel protected.

How can I keep painting Pain as a friend? She just is. The fear she showed me made her worth all my energy. I mean, fear of the Pain of losing those you love, the Pain of feeling vulnerable. Pain is a reminder that I wasn't safe. I'm not safe. She reminds me that I long for unconditional love and safety, but I will never have it, so I should be afraid. When I listen to Pain, I remember that I want to feel safe. And I believe that staying with her means safety.

"You are beautiful you know," she whispered as she gently brushed my hair back behind my ear. "Look at what you can endure alone."

"I hear you," I said. "Though I don't feel alone when you're here. I feel alive again somehow." My nerve endings awakened as I whispered back to her.

Pound made me feel like I couldn't actually feel. Not without him. He was so jarring. The shock of him made me numb. Pain woke me up. Pain was a companion where Pound was mean. Pain was never mean. She was just alert. Present.

I was alert.

You might forget by now that Pain is a monster. She made me believe that fear was safety, and if I didn't stay with her in fear, Pound would return.

Pound returned regardless. He made a home in my chest, whether Pain followed or not. He always found his way back to me. And I had a manner of missing him.

3

Two Was a Short Breath

Why should I allow myself to feel safe in a world that gives me so many reasons to be afraid?

I mentioned Pain was a friend. Did you forget that she was a monster? Pain is the one who shows up most often in my nightmares, by my bedside. She stays close, as compassion would, but her smile is terrifying. Pain's smile tells you the truth of her intentions, which are always to hurt. I said I would tell you about her face, and I realize now that I was distracted by her hand and how her fingers feel while intertwined with mine–tight, gripping. Safe.

Pain's face is chilling to behold, though hers doesn't change as much as Pound's. Now that I think about it, her face doesn't change at all. She always looks the same. Best friends should feel familiar. Pain's face is familiar. I can't see her very well at night, but I know that she's smiling. In the blur of the darkness, I have mistaken her shape for that of my husband or the ghost of my grandfather—people I trust who are both here and gone to another dimension. Pain finds me in all dimensions. When I wake up and see her, I'm screaming. Memories of Pound. She reminds me then that I should be afraid of Pound and I need her. Although I know in those horrifying moments that I should fear her. I am screaming because I know she's wrong, though she's given every breath she owns to convince me that she's right. Like a best friend would.

Pain is not really my friend. She is a monster. I see her at night because I have nightmares. Another reminder that monsters are real. In the night, I can see them for who they are. Pound bangs on my chest when I wake to Pain. Her smiling face and floating figure quickly disappear as my eyes adjust to the darkness outside my nightmares. But I can still feel her circled around my body, coiling like a snake, trying to lull me into believing she is protecting me. Some people call Pain and Pound "night terrors." Night terrors are my body's reminder that monsters are real. Someone told me once that I shake at night, quivering like a cornered mouse. Pain squeezed me so tightly I didn't notice that I shook. I see Pain and remember that she's dangerous, and Pound won't let me fall back asleep when she disappears. The more my eyes focus on her in the darkness, the more she tries to hide. Pain is good at hiding, which is why I can't sleep at night. I know she's never really gone.

I can train my mind to ignore, maybe even transcend, Pain. Wouldn't that be something? But how can I transcend beyond the supernatural? Beyond a creature that will never really disappear? The truth that I cling to in my heart is that monsters cannot be mastered if they still exist. Do you think there's another lesson I need to learn? Nightmares don't have to disappear in order for me to master them. Maybe now, I realize, there is something I could consider. Monsters can continue to exist, and I can master them. Mastery begins with memory. Let me remember the sound of their voices. Pound again.

"Knock, Baby. Knock, knock, knock." I don't just hear Pound—I feel him too. Mostly, in my skin, breath, and chest. "I am strong, Love. You are stronger with me too," his voice is gentle and gruff sometimes, a soft strength. "I can protect you from all the other monsters, like Pain. Remember how lonely you feel without her? With me, you won't be alone. Let me follow you. Let me lie with you. Wake to My protection."

Pound pretends.

He wants to sound like a friend.

Now I remember. He acts as if Pain is his enemy, but they are born of the same. Pain follows him, but that doesn't mean she isn't as strong. She simply thrives in emptiness. Empty is all that remains when Pound leaves. God, I keep coming back to Pain. What the hell? Pound is so loud, but Pain is who I fear and love the most. That fear is why I can't stop talking about her. I fixate the most on Pain. She circles my mind, even when I think she's gone. The monster I fixate on has mastered me. So let me share more of my master's voice with you. I like to recall her words and dance with them in my memory. I hear her all the time, "You are stronger when you are lonely. Pound can't find you here. Fear doesn't exist in Pain. In me. Don't you feel how I numb you? If you are numb, you've escaped."

What a beautiful song Pain sings. A numbing lullaby.

If I am numb, then I've escaped. Matter of fact, no, I haven't. Where am I if I am numb? To live with Pain is to freeze. Numbness doesn't erase Pain. It just makes you feel like her presence is a comfort. But she's underneath and around, becoming that much stronger. Feeding on my anxious energy. She needs me. If I am unaware that she's there, she becomes stronger. There were many years I slept alone with Pain, confident that Pound was gone, becoming so numb to her touch I forgot how tightly she clung to my skin. Then one night, he returned, and now I remember that she was there whispering, protecting me.

Pound rang the doorbell on the night he came back. The sound pounded through my home at 3:00 a.m., ringing through the darkness.

Ding-dong, he rang once.

I heard him.

He's loud.

I heard him and my heart jumped. I was instantly awake. Pound is terrifying because he can change his shape. I didn't know what to look for this time. I just knew to avoid the door.

"Freeze," Pain whispered. "Listen." She spoke softly.

"He'll ring again," I told her. I know he will.

"Then freeze so he can't find you. Stay here in bed with me. The curtains are closed. Don't move and he won't find you." Her voice was soft and protective.

"You're right," I told her. "Pound changes his appearance, but he feels the same. I know it's him at the door. Or could it be Her?"

"Her?" Pain whispered. "Who is She?"

"She is a different kind of monster…one bigger and stranger than Pound. I don't know what She looks like, only that I am certain She will come around."

"I think I know who you mean," Pain whispered with something like recognition and foreboding in her voice. "I've smelled Her near before when my jabs at you were sharpest."

My gut ached for a moment, remembering Pain's warnings, recalling the secret threat. Then I shook my head and said, "No matter who is at the door, I am certain there's danger. It has to be a monster. You've taught me to freeze, so I will."

Ding-dong. Louder.

Ding-dong! Louder Pound rang.

"Pound. Pound. Pound!"

Before I knew what happened, Pound was in my chest. The door didn't matter anymore because Pound found a way in. I still tried to hide from him, though he was already inside. I was desperate not to let him see me.

I searched the darkness for Pain, but she was silent. "Are you sure the curtains are closed?" I whispered in desperation. Whispering was the host of our companionship; of course, she would respond. "Is there any crack in the shades? We can't let him in!"

Pain didn't answer. I never saw if Pound was actually at the door. But he was in my chest, and Pain was gone. I was left shaking in my bed. My nerves were on fire. And I was with Pound.

Pound whispered to me in the darkness, trying to sound like Pain. His voice was deep, certain, and almost soft for once. "You'll never have enough without me. No one makes you feel like I do. Pain left you in the darkness alone. But I was here. Remember that next time she comes around. Live in fear with me," he said with as comforting a voice as monsters can muster. "Without fear, there is no safety."

I had to think a lot around Pound. I couldn't speak much with him. He didn't want to hear my voice the way Pain did. Pain's voice felt like my own. But at this moment, Pain was gone.

Pound was here. He reminded me that "Fear is the only safe place. With me, you know what's coming. Through all the years, you know what's coming when I'm here. Fear teaches you to expect. Let me comfort you."

I retreated into myself as Pound spoke. The space in my chest where he Pounded was shrinking. The Pounding slowed and almost felt like a steady beat. I began to feel at home with him. I laid back down in the midst of the quiet Pounds. For a moment, I thought I heard another voice somewhere, though I didn't know who or what that voice was—I couldn't name the tone, but I could hear the words, "You are afraid of living in fear. Yet you are afraid all the time. Is this anticipatory purgatory home? Or are you in more danger?"

Who are you? I thought. Then my heart started pounding again.

This unfamiliar voice felt new, strange, and threatening. But wait…

Did I know this voice?

There was something familiar and nonthreatening about the question too. My heart started pounding again, and I lost my thoughts as each one began to race incoherently...

"Run."

"Don't trust."

"Find comfort in Pound."

"No, don't! Remember his angry eyes? Bloodshot and sick."

"Pound is sick."

"He needs help."

"I can't give him that help."

"But should I?"

"Pound helps me forget Him."

"The danger helps me forget Him."

"I'm not afraid..."

"I'm not afraid..."

"I'm NOT afraid."

"Fear has consumed me. Fear is all I am. I will welcome the shaking."

1

Creation is powerful. The world created monstrous beings for me, and my mind made them my own. I found power when I realized the monsters were their own, and they were my creations. In an effort to survive Pain and Pound, my instincts were activated and they built upon themselves. Lightning bolts connecting my brain's roots. Lightning is stunning. I was stunned. Some may believe that instincts are primitive; humans should exist as something higher. But I became more powerful when I learned my instincts were all the higher and more powerful versions of myself. Well, the self I discovered when I believed I was in danger. When I ran from Pound and embraced Pain, we created something together. We made something quickly. Danger leads to the misfortune of twisted memories. I cannot remember how I responded to and created Pain and Pound, but there was something profound in how quickly they appeared and how quickly I worked alongside them. The creation of instinct is quick, responding to a threat in seconds is admirable.

"Pound!"

"Wait, what?" I was thinking in the morning after sleeping with Pound, believing I was comforted. Believing that Pound wanted quiet. *Isn't quiet why he tried to sound like Pain?* My thoughts were interrupted by the very same monster who rocked me to sleep.

"Pound!"

"Where was he coming from?" My mind raced…

He was in my chest, but I don't feel him there now.

Then his eyes appeared before me again. I could see his eyes but not the face he chose this time. I saw the redness in Pound's eyes when stared at me. Now I knew what to call the red.

"Rage."

Pound paced this time too. His body wouldn't stop moving as he spewed rage. "I can't say anything because then I'm a narcissistic asshole! You're right. I'm not allowed to speak. I'm a monster!"

Couldn't he hear himself? Why can't he feel that he's screaming? Why is he back now? I don't understand his rage. And I don't want the rage pointed at me again. In the midst of my fear, I realized that I didn't want to be ashamed. And Pound always made me feel ashamed. I realized that when I finally recognized his monstrous face.

Why am I the target? I asked myself, but I didn't ask Pound. Not yet. My whole life, I believed I should be the target.

He (not Pound but He) taught me I should be ashamed.

I deserve to be the target, I thought. I am fulfilling my destiny if I am the target. I should be ashamed.

Pound makes me feel ashamed. I can live the truth that his rage is "my fault." I am doing the right thing.

Then I started to recognize Pound as a monster. The monster was human and something else all at once. I knew no other response to him other than screaming and silence. Screaming is the language of monsters, so I screamed first…

"Leave me alone!" My voice rang high and furious.

"Right, because I'm a monster!" Pound questioned, fury fuming in his voice, but a cold realization was floating in the sound too. A realization that Pound didn't want to face.

I didn't believe Pound was only a monster this time. He was something else too. But his words and his rage were the language of monsters. I felt confused, and in my confusion, I just wanted him to leave.

"Go," I commanded.

He lingered.

"Pound, go!" My voice softened from screaming but still sounded stern.

I remembered that angry shouts do not encourage monsters to calm their rage. Returning their anger only fuels more fury. Sometimes I forgot this lesson when I spoke the monster language.

"Fine, I'll go. You're better off without me anyway!" Pound's voice was still furious but began to fade. "I know what you're thinking. I know what I am. You'd rather find someone else anyway! You'll never hear me scream again!"

I just wanted Pound to stop yelling. I just wanted him to go. There was no comfort in the fear I felt around him anymore. Rage didn't feel right. Rage didn't feel like all that existed.

"You're hurting me, Pound. You're scaring me."

The rage in his eyes softened as I said, "You're scaring me." He didn't go quietly. He paced more and lightly slammed the door. I knew he wasn't coming back inside this time. Not tonight. He left me with Pain. She appeared at my bedside as I curled up into myself after Pound slammed the door.

Pain stared at me, but she was inside me too. She felt like a thick rock in my throat, a stone that slid down into my chest. Pain was heavy in my body and warm in my eyes.

"I ran from Pound," I whispered to her.

"What did he look like this time?"

"I still can't describe his face, but this time, he turned his hat backwards."

"What about his eyes?" she gently whispered.

"Not blue anymore but rage in them again."

"Ah. Rage. I know how he fuels Pound. I've seen both of them before. I'm sorry, Love. Did he smell like whiskey again?"

"Yes."

"I'm not surprised. Oh, I am so sorry." She lightly grazed my shoulders with her fingers as I curled up in bed. "And how do you feel?" she asked softly.

"The worst part of Pound is he always makes me feel crazy. I question everything. All my choices. All of who I am. But the questions don't feel like growth. The questions are isolating. The questions make me hate myself."

"I don't know what you mean by growth but keep talking to me. Keep talking to yourself. Sit alone in these thoughts. Don't let them leave this room. You're safe in isolation," Pain cooed.

I believed Pain and kept talking, "Pound came back inside someone who made me feel safe, alive most of the time, in a way no amount of adrenaline could. He hurt me so badly."

Pain wrapped her heavy arms around me as I spoke of hurting. She held me. Her presence held me when Pound left me empty. Heavy felt like whole.

"You're all right," Pain whispered. "I'm here. The angry giant is gone. He left you alone. He left you alone with me. Pound knows that you deserve me, so he created the space with his empty knocking. Shh... You don't have to use your voice anymore. You know the sounds won't land anywhere. Just listen to me whisper. Let me remind you why you are better off alone with me. I can shelter you. Rest in Pain. I can help you forget the fear Pound caused. Just hurt. Let me sink in. Pain is better than empty."

I fell asleep with Pain beside me. She held me throughout the night as I awoke periodically and remembered she was there, with her hand firmly draped across my stomach.

2

In the morning, Pain felt wrong.

In that sense, I was also awakened to another voice, quiet but real, "I'm here too. I won't force you to listen to me, but if you do, you might find that you feel better."

"Pain?" I asked, not believing that someone else could exist with her.

"No, I am not Pain. It's okay that she's here. You need her sometimes, even though she is a monster. I just want to let you know that she doesn't need to be your best friend."

"Who are you?" I asked.

"You saw me yesterday when you thought you were alone. You were under the heat of the sun, staring at the blue sky. Then as your eyes gazed downward, you saw me rooted in the garden."

"I remember the garden. Where were you?"

"I was near the dark-purple flower, the iris. A deep purple you may not have a name for yet. When you saw me, you stood up and walked to me."

"I remember walking and the sun. I felt my heart beating loudly. The heat helped me feel every pulse of my blood."

"Yes, I was there. I know that you feel Pound in your chest, but I am alongside Pound too. He may seem like less of an enemy when you know that your own life beats beside him."

"What do you mean?"

"Your heart. The pounding of your chest carries blood to your body, and not every pound means danger. Pounding means life too. You have strength in your blood."

"I don't fully understand, but something tells me you are right. But where were you in the garden? Were you the flower?"

"I was the tiny burst of bright purple that you noticed in the flower. Remember when you leaned in closely, taking the time to see me? The tiny, fuzzy hat of brightness on the flower's petal. The one you never noticed before. I was in the flower and in your eyes. I exist because you saw me, and now you hear me."

"What do I have to do with any of this?"

"You have everything to do with all of this."

"Can we name 'this'?"

"Not yet. But I and 'this' and you, We are something like hope. And We can exist at the same time as the monsters. We have existed at the same time as the monsters."

"We."

3

WE

Pain's rocks were still in my stomach, but her arm wasn't draped around me anymore. She simply pinched lightly as I thought of We. I didn't understand who We was at that moment, but I started thinking about Pain and noticed a small shift. My body felt a little lighter.

"It's okay that she's here," I remembered We's words.

I loved Pain, but I wanted to run from her. I believed I would only ever find freedom on the day that I could finally abandon Pain in my bed and on the side of the roads we walked together so many times. But We said Pain could stay, "She doesn't have to be your best friend." Who is Pain if not my best friend? Does We know her? Does We know Pound? I let sadness sit in my eyes as I felt Pain pinching and feared that We wasn't real. I allowed tears to form naturally. I didn't pull them back or force more to fall. Pain sometimes told me to force or pull tears, depending on where I was. I let the tears form into sadness and wondered what would happen if I allowed sadness to make me feel powerful instead of vulnerable. Pound inspired sadness. I sensed that there was a reason beyond the hurt he caused, but I didn't know what that reason was either. A few more tears fell as I sat alone. The tears didn't feel the same as when Pain commanded them… Pain. I imagined how it might feel to let go of her hand but allow her around. Where was I now with Pain and Pound?

I thought of We and let my mind slip into a different place, one that wasn't cold, a place where I didn't shake. I began wandering under the sun, near the purple irises We whispered of. In this sunny place, I thought of my last argument with Pound. I remembered his cold eyes as he towered over my bedside, his clenched fists pulsing with fury. Instead of running, I chose to keep looking at him. What else could I see in Pound? What appeared beyond my fear?

We spoke again, "When you're in a room with monsters, you're never the only one they see. When you argue with a monster, you're arguing with every monster they've ever heard, every word they've ever learned to spit back in defense. Monsters are only focused on defending. Defense is the pattern formed in their brains. Automatic. Autopilot. Survival. If you look closely at a monster's eyes, especially during times of misalignment, you can see that they are lost in their minds."

I recalled the blood in Pound's eyes. In my memory, outside of my fear and the wake of his fury, I finally saw that he was looking beyond me as he pounded and screamed in my direction. Pound was wearing wounds from a monster who screamed and pounded at him. Perhaps Pound was seeing many monsters. After Pound left, I thought about his words, "You're better off without me." Maybe Pound isn't so arrogant. Maybe Pound is self-deprecating. He hurts to defend. My thoughts of Pound softened. I set them aside and promised to hold them in my hand later. Naturally, my mind turned then in the direction of Pain.

So now I remember the road, a place where I might have abandoned Pain. The irony is that she once saved my life on the road. Or I thought she did. I was running, Pain was alongside me. He had broken my heart. I was empty and angry. My eyes were blurred with Pain's tears as she screamed with me and we drove into the night.

Furiously.

"I hate you!" Pain and I screamed together. Childish maybe, but I felt rage as a tantrum, and Pain justified rage.

"You should hate Him!" She blared. "Look what He has done! Look how He has shamed you! The very heart He praised and skin He glorified He now calls a temptation. You are a beautiful creation, and He called you a temptation! 'Maybe I'm Paul?' He said. My ass. He didn't seem to care about Paul's righteousness when he was grabbing yours!"

"You're right." My throat burned as my eyes flooded with tears, blurring the road before me.

"Run," Pain's voice rang. "Run! Run off the road! Keep screaming and run! You'll show Him if you're dead. He'll see the damage He's done!"

"You're right." My voice was still raised. "Screaming speaks. If I'm dead, I speak. And anyway, I don't know how to live with a heart that's this broken. Where do I live when I handed my creator my heart as I was instructed, only to find that He would squeeze the life out of me? I watched my blood drip through his clenching fist. If I am dead, He will know how wrong He was to squeeze my heart, constricting me like a snake."

Then I remembered another voice where before I had only recalled Pain.

"He's wrong."

"Pain?"

The voice wasn't Pain. And the voice wasn't Him.

She slowly slipped through my arm and gripped the wheel. She was in my veins, steadying my hand, speaking in my head.

"Don't run this way," the voice was soft but firm. She didn't scream.

"Hello?" My eyes still burned with tears, and Pain gripped the wheel, forcing my steering to jerk to the right and left, the exit ramp circling wildly in my fists.

"You know He's wrong."

I felt her gently slide through my fingers as she spoke. She was a peaceful spirit sinking inside my own body, steadying me. "Don't be ashamed of screaming. You're not wrong to scream. And you're just not wrong. You do not need to be ashamed. You are not shame. Hold your grip. Don't run."

I heard her. I listened. But I didn't let her into my conscious mind. I listened, but I wanted to keep screaming with Pain. I didn't know then that the voice was We.

We might have been me. A beautiful ghost in my hand. A light spirit, calming my nerves, a coolness in the fire. Pain leaned her head back on the passenger seat, bouncing back up slightly, like that of a child who had given up her fight for a fast-food dinner, accepting something healthier, knowing the truth that healthy was right. I might have heard Pain breathe, or maybe the sound was a sigh.

Yes, Pain took a deep breath. Pain was quelled when We spoke. I remembered.

"I knew she was right."

My memory was interrupted.

"It's Pain," her voice was piercing but soft.

Pain looked at me and stopped pinching my stomach. She let go. Her smile began to fade into something neutral or maybe something sad.

"I remember We," Pain sighed. "She is not a ghost. But she moves as one."

"She floats, doesn't she, Pain?"

"She floats and she lets me scream. But I want to stop screaming when she speaks."

"Why?"

"Because I don't want you to die."

My eyes were full of my own tears. Sadness and compassion mingled, swimming together. Compassion began to form in my stomach too, but it didn't pierce like Pain. I just started to feel full.

"What do you mean, Pain?"

Pain's scary smile fully faded. I could see that she felt sad. "I scare you to keep you alive. If I stop, you won't be safe."

"Then why do you listen to We?"

"Because I understand that I don't know when to stop scaring you."

My heart beat the way it pounded when Pound was present. I felt alert, as if I were under the sun, not afraid. "Pain?"

She gently tossed her hair. I could finally see her eyes. Beautiful strands of brown and green, like mine, weaving together under the sun.

"I don't want you to die." Her mouth quivered and three tears fell.

Tears like mine.

I understood then that Pain had never left me. And maybe I didn't know her as well as I thought. Maybe she had been compassion as well as Pain all along. Maybe We knew she should stay. Maybe Pain had been learning when to scream. And in her quiet moments, I thought she disappeared.

Pain had tried to save my daughter's life too, the same one that carried Pound's disease. The needles poked, pierced, and prodded her since she was three. But the pain in the needles was trying to save her too. I am learning that the line between Pain and compassion is very thin. Maybe there is no line at all; they just need to honor each other's time. I searched my memory further and noticed that I often felt compassion when I saw Pain hiding inside another human.

She was my best friend, so I always recognized her, and compassion always followed.

Pain had a heart. She made me think about fear. I spent so much time fearing Pain; I never realized until I spoke with her in that moment that she was afraid too.

1

Fear. Why was I so afraid of the monsters? I panicked when Pound was around, in my chest and in my town. I couldn't breathe when Pain was near. Her grip on me was suffocating. Yet I loved them both. Up until this moment, I believed "there is no fear in love." He quoted that in His book. But I guess I never really understood fear, nor did I understand love. I only knew that they couldn't exist together as I was taught.

But was I taught the truth?

Let me look at fear for a second. I see Pain and Pound's eyes. Pain intentionally hid her eyes behind her hair. Pound's were blinded by red. Both monsters were hiding. Before, I believed Pain was born from Pound. Now I realize he had hidden in her more than I knew. She may have existed before. Pain wrapped her arms around him too. She was trying to protect him, and he was attempting to ignore her. The red was a sign that Pound was protecting himself, pounding so loudly that he couldn't feel Pain around him.

Both Pain and Pound had something to lose. And they had already lost a lot.

Or believed they had.

Fear of losing. I was afraid alongside them. I was afraid of losing. I opened my door to Pound because I thought I had lost. His pounding drowned out the shame I believed I was weaving. The shame where He left me.

2

I would like to tell you who He is. Though I know now you might be focused on Pound. I don't fully understand Pound yet, only that he might be friends with Pain, even though he ignores her. I've ignored my friends before too. But I understand Him now. I understand how Pain and Pound helped me run from Him too. I was taught about Him before I was old enough to remember where He began, when I was young and my memory was new. I was told He loved me unconditionally but only if I was ashamed. His voice was in the sky, in congregations, in leaders painted as compassion, and all around my family. His voice was in my head, pushing me to run with Pain and toward Pound, so I would need Him. I would like to show you how He sounds, "Rest in Me. Feel whole in Me. My arms are open. You are a fractured and depraved being, you know. You need Me to be whole."

"It feels good to reach toward You, but why am I grasping at nothing?"

"Are you questioning Me? Are you doubting My existence?"

"I—"

"If you are questioning, you should be ashamed of that too," His voice was stern.

It felt strange to be told to stop asking questions.

"Rely on Me. Don't question! If you choose to question, you will be lost."

"Oh." Sadness rested in my voice as I sighed and looked down. "I guess I am lost."

"You were born lost. But the good news is, you can try to find yourself in Me. Even if you don't hear or see Me. Inability to see and hear is your weak human nature doubting. Run from your human nature. Cast your sin away."

"What is sin?"

"You are sin. Everything that weaves through your being is sin. You were crafted that way. It is in your nature to hurt, hide, and steal. But please, good news, I will help you heal."

"Oh no, that's awful." My heart ached. Then my legs began to quake.

"Fall on your knees. Worship me. Your submission will feel good. I promise you'll see."

"Okay, I'm sure I will." I longed for peace.

This being in the sky and all around me said He was peace. He was everyone around me, they all believed. So I should too.

I did.

But then I learned He was wrong. He was empty. I started to see. Now I know that vision of peace was We, though I didn't recognize her. He separated me from myself. In his eyes, Pain and Pound became monsters. And I embraced the monsters only to make Him angry. I didn't see who the monsters were, only that they frustrated Him.

I wanted Him to feel angry. He made me feel ashamed. He made me believe I should be ashamed for existing as I was. "Human." "Weak." I was angry too—though anger is never a good reason to befriend monsters.

"Can I interrupt for a moment?" a light voice whispered.

"We?"

"Yes, We are here. We were there when He was too, though he tried to drown Us out. When you were drowning in Him, We let Pain scream. She helped you run from Him as you needed to. You ran because who you really needed was you. He wouldn't let you hear yourself. Do you know why?"

"Yes, He told me to live in shame, so one day I'd meet him in the sky."

"That's right. How can you expect to know yourself as the creator you are when He whispered to you that you are shame? What other kind of life would a creative mind weave then? You created yourself in shame to please Him. Your motives were only to belong. Then when He left you empty, the agony pierced because it was prolonged."

"So what you're saying is, I should seek something new?"

"Yes and keep trying to see the monsters too."

3

I thought about what We said, "Keep seeing the monsters too." Then I thought of my own idea, *create something new*. Could I be a creator? Had I been throughout my entire life? Even if I was a monster too? I spent some time thinking about Pain and Pound. Their eyes were a mystery to me, yet the monsters swam in my own irises. My eyes felt heavy with them. I searched my memory deeper. When was I Pain?

I was Pain when I lied. I was a creator then too. Sometimes, liars are the best creators, though their pieces pierce instead of promoting peace.

How did I lie?

I was in Pain. I became Pain as she sought to protect me. I pursued Pain in others yet numbed myself as the cause. I was angry at the many Pounds. I was angry at Him. I was angry at men. So I hurt the men I could, believing that becoming Pain and luring Pain to haunt them would give me power.

Let me count, *One, two, three, four, five… Too many more. Too many faces I numbed myself to while living as Pain. What did I tell them?*

"Sure, I love you. Of course I do. I miss you." What a fun story.

Stories on the water. Stories in the wind. Stories down channels weaving in and around lily pads. Stories in campers and driveways, old couches and tall front doors. Stories in cars, pretending they were an escape. In all these places, in all these people, I lied to feed my pride. I was in Pain, and I caused Pain, but what a beautiful story I made them believe. Or at least I made them believe my conditional love was worth lying to themselves to believe.

What a twisted web. Lying, cheating, pretending. Lies were my creation and they are creation, and maybe there could be some beauty in that truth. But beauty is not the end of lying and all the stories. In the end, lies are lies. And the more I lied, the more I became Pain, a more dangerous kind of monster because I could lie. And what I have learned of Pain is that her primary instinct is to protect.

"De-fense! De-fense!" Listen as Pain and I cheer.

What a team, Pain and I. I feel sorry for the victories we won together. I feel sorry for the Pain we caused, believing we were justified if the men showed a shred of Pound's nature or welcomed our lies because they believed someday I would honor them with the truth.

I am sorry.

4

Stories are so powerful. Pain is powerful. I am too. I am powerful with Pain as her and alone. I want to know more of what that power could do if befriending Pain, becoming Pain, and creating more Pain weren't my goals. What about the pastimes where she was present but not my focus? Not my best friend…

I served. Not servitude but genuine creation and gratitude. I can smell spices. Paprika, Cajun, garlic, and black pepper. I created for them. I cooked delicious sauces, vegetables, and meats. I don't think I care much for meat now. Seems too violent. But I created peace with spices. Not out of servitude, but because I loved blending flavors, relaxing into the moment of a meal. I learned to cook when I was Pain. I learned to grow when I was Pain.

I see gardens too. Flowers with the same bright sparks, the fireworks We reminded me of. I planted gardens with others who were in Pain, others who frequently became Pound. They were young men. They attended a school I served. Pound and violence knew them well. They told me how they were welcomed into gangs as long-lost family members.

"Your parents don't love you? They left you out here? How cruel," the leaders whispered like wolves. "Well, we run in packs here. We'll take you in. But remember, we provide for each other. We have food. We have shelter. We have belonging too. Run this money. Shoot this gun. Stand in front of us. That's all you have to do. The human on the other end doesn't matter as long as we're with you."

Then the young men told me how they paid the price. Bullet scars scraped across their ribs. Mistaken drive-bys. Robberies they were commanded to commit. Cells with cold bars and apathetic guards. They were in Pain and they were Pound. Pain and Pound were the heads of household, and the young men were just following orders.

I told stories; I lived Pain. I was losing my home and the young men had lost theirs. For me, divorce. For them, "criminal conduct." We were all in Pain, and we all found a garden. The plants were tools for learning. Grow the seeds inside then watch them sprout in the spring. So many bright marigolds. Spiderweb bursts of orange, yellow, and red, all woven together in bunches of flowers. Families. The young men and I dug into the earth; we met the soil that offered to nourish the plants. The dirt felt healthy in our hands. We were creating with the earth even as we were in Pain. Many of us screamed and hid in the hallways of the school. Pound was knocking and pushed the instinct to protect on them. But all of us grew. All of us saw the earth. We were healing together more than we knew.

1

What I know about Pain now is that she doesn't disappear. She didn't then and she won't now. But Pain wasn't my best friend when I was with the men and the marigolds. She was there, but We were learning that we didn't have to scream. We learned about screaming. We learned that the sound could awaken Pound.

"Okay, Pound, here we go."

"What, Alex? What do you want!" He stared deeply into my eyes.

"You're acting like a child!" I faced his fury toe to toe.

Pound only became angrier. "Whatever, Alex. I know more than you."

My stomach lurched with Pain, and I felt Pound in my chest too. Maybe this time, I should listen to my own Pound. Maybe he has more to offer than I knew.

I stopped raising my voice to the Pound in front of me and closed my eyes to listen to the one inside.

"Hi," he whispered.

I didn't know Pound could be so quiet. His voice was a tenor, a little raspy but not gruff.

"Hi, Pound."

He felt like a friend too. "I want to ask you a question."

"I'm ready for you."

"Why do children scream? Why do they yell?"

"They want our attention. But sometimes, that knowledge is hard to tell."

"That's right, Alex. Can you think more?"

"I've been trying to think lately. Maybe there's more to you pounding at my door."

"My anger is misplaced. I will give you that. My pounding hurts. I won't deny facts. You said you were sorry, and I am too."

"What more can I learn from you?"

"Babies scream because they need. Thirst, hunger, (Pain is with them too), discomfort, and loneliness. They want to be held and screaming is their only choice for a voice."

"I have heard babies scream. My heart fills with anxiety at the sound."

"Anxiety, yes, the sound is like sandpaper. But what other option have they?"

"None that I know of, I suppose."

"Children scream too, just like the adult Pounds you knew. Attention and protection are their pursuits."

"I can understand that."

"And We can learn to use our voices without screaming. Though sometimes, humans need to be heard. Pain needs to be heard when she screams. Humans can raise their voices to protect." Pound's voice softened as he spoke.

"So why does your screaming terrify me?"

"Because when I have screamed at you, the time wasn't right to protect."

"De-fense. De-fense."

"Yes, you, Pain, and I are on the same team. Though when We scream at each other, We feel like enemies. Would you give me a moment to show you when my pounding protected? If I show you, maybe you can discern the difference between protection, attention, and danger."

"Yes, you can show me."

"Find me in your mind."

2

When I Stopped Breathing

Pain and I played with fire once. Really, Pain and I played more like one, two, three, four, five, six, seven…eight times. I might have lost count. We played with a Pound so dangerous I'd call him Death. This Death was how I knew to expect the She-Death Monster. But Her story is later… Now that I know Pain better, I don't remember her beside me with Death. She found Death with me. Near him was the only time I heard her scream in my head. I remember him, and I hear her scream. Pain's scream faded, and my chest pounded. I wasn't alone. Pound appeared in my chest when I met Death, and Pain faded.

I see fire. I knew from the moment I saw Death that he was dangerous. Pound was knocking from the inside when I looked at Death. Now I know Pound was warning me. Death's eyes weren't red like Pound's. When Death was looking at me, he looked through eyes of his own. A monster's. Wide. Blue. Round. Suffocating. I gripped Death's eyes like a coal in my hand. He burned until I could feel again. I was too numb; Pain had been my best friend for too long. I wanted to shut her out.

Pound became desperate, "Pound, Pound, Pound!" Louder in my chest. I ignored him. Death was the only time I couldn't feel Pain draped around me. Now I know she was screaming in my head all the while. Even she couldn't let Death see her. She had to hide and scream to keep me alive. And Pound was still at my door, only this time, he was sweating, knocking desperately to get me to open and see. Still, ignored.

It was I who wanted to die.

I knew Death could kill me. I knew a part of him wanted to. I still know it. I felt his hand slide slowly across my throat, and his calloused skin comforted me. No, it wasn't me who craved comfort in Death. I don't know what I was.

Numb.

I was so numb I played with fire. I ignored myself and crashed into me at the same time.

I embraced Death.

But he didn't kill me.

I still don't know why.

"We do."

"We…Pain, Pound, You, and We."

"Your patterns of survival were already killing you. We were accidentally killing you and saving you. Death wasn't as unfamiliar as he seemed."

"Well then, how am I alive?"

"You have wings. You flew away."

I looked down at my side and saw feathers near my hips. Clearly, the tips of wings that were attached at the middle of my back. Thick and strong like an angel's. Wings are the creation of monsters. Then I felt their roots between my shoulder blades, the high center of my back where I held stress. Now I know that where I carried stress I was building muscles. The muscles of my wings. I had been flexing them without knowing. Flexing with Pain and Pound.

"Death can't fly," We whispered.

"And you didn't really want to die…"

"There is more to you than you knew. You saw Death's dangerous eyes and you flew."

"He knew he couldn't catch you."

"Maybe he was a monster. But you are a dove. Your heart was always in the sky. He can't reach you up above."

"He or Death?"

"Both."

"But why did I want to die?"

"Sometimes the world We see simply can't hold our hearts."

"Why did I fly?"

"You have your own reasons. But you also knew he wanted to eat your wings."

I lost track of who was speaking. Me, Pain, Pound, or all of us? We.

3

I Learn to Catch My Breath

He wanted to eat my wings. That's a scary thought. Gross too. Ew. Well, now I am confused. I could be a creator. I am. What has made me believe I am not? What have I created that made me believe the monsters should be my best friends? That their reality was the only one?

Fear.

I created fear. Pain and Pound helped me weave Fear's wings. The wings I saw rooted in me now were not woven of Fear; they were something else. But Fear had helped me fly before. Not above, not into air and light, only flight.

The wings I made with Pain, Pound, and Fear froze me to the ground. Jagged wings of ice. They grew under my feet and froze my veins. In flight I was actually frozen, eyes darting back and forth, frantically searching where to run. I realize now that Fear was a monster too. The most powerful one.

Fear commanded Pain and Pound. She beat in my very blood. Every choice, every creation, every word, wrought of Fear. I believed when I was bolted to the earth, frozen in my wings of Fear, that I was moving fast. I believed I was always moving, racing. Running to safety. But I was actually going nowhere, except round and round in Fear's wheel. Fear etched Pound's face in my irises. She whispered that he was always there. I should always be afraid of Pound. I should never understand him.

If I understand, if I slow down, then I am giving in. Pound will own me, and I'll lose myself.

Fear spoke to me of "I." She is the "I" that whispered to me of Death. The "I" that wanted to die. I didn't have to be afraid if I was dead.

Pound is a monster. That's always been true. But there was more to Pound. Fear simply would not let me see. But now that I can look Fear in the face, I see that she is a cold block of ice that I want to chip away so I can find Pound behind her.

"Pound, Pound, Pound!" I called as I chipped away at Fear, pounding to reach the monster I had so often run from. I broke the ice away and saw Pound that day, his unchanging face bursting out of the cold night.

Pound's skin is light; he's tall and bright. His face glistens with sweat. His hair is black, clean cut, and jagged, trimmed short around his ears so he can always hear himself. Pound's eyes have been blue, but they are dark too, and brown eyes are what I see before me. Though I notice now that Fear is melting, Pound really was always the same; she had simply skewed my perception of his face.

The wings of ice melted under my feet. Pound stood before me, and I stood firm. As I took a moment to look at him, I saw that his fists were clenched and his forehead drenched. Ready to furiously pound. Pound huffed and puffed, his arms and shoulders moving up and down like an angry ape.

"Don't look at me!" he screamed.

I relaxed my eyes. Then thought for a moment, *What if Pound didn't mean what he screamed? If he didn't want to be noticed, why did he yell so loudly?*

"I don't yell!" Pound raised his voice.

Then I remembered what I'd learned about attention. Pound had my attention, but maybe he wanted something more. As a monster running from a monster, I had never known how to answer the door. I looked at Pound's eyes for a moment, and his irises began to turn gray. Then I recalled my conversation with We. Pound wasn't looking at me when he screamed. He saw a different monster, one who appeared as a ghost.

"I don't see the ghost who gripped your hand, the one who saved you when you ran."

"Who do you see, Pound?"

"I see what I should be. And I smell burned toast."

"I am no stranger to burning. And I know 'Should Be.' But what does Should Be mean to you?"

Pound finally relaxed his shoulders and started to breathe. I could see in his eyes there was a memory.

"I knew a Pound once, long before I knocked on your door. He broke what I knew of 'We.'"

"What makes you so special?" he spat at me, my own Pound. "What makes you think you could be? I dreamed of fireworks like you, Alex. The kind you saw in the iris flower. I wrote stories and saw through eyes without Fear. I saw Pain in others. I relaxed them with my patience. Before they'd sleep, I'd paint pictures of beauty, hope, and mountains in their heads."

Pound was a painter, a sandman sailing through human dreams. Where there was trauma, darkness, and anger, he helped the dreamers float along as if on a channel somewhere serene.

I looked at Pound and saw channels, beautiful rivers with light glowing in the night. Stars swam in his eyes as they relaxed into a deeper brown.

"Do you still paint, Pound?"

"My name isn't Pound, it's Rayne."

Pound was still drenched but no longer in sweat. His arms and legs flowed like water, a figure of beautiful, flowing motion he became.

"I'm not becoming. I have always been. And honestly, so have We."

I thought about Rayne's words for a moment and started to understand what it meant to be free.

In the past, Pound and I had seen each other through eyes of Fear. Everyone is a monster when you're afraid.

"I screamed because I believed I'm not good enough," Rayne whispered. "My own Pound made me believe it was so. I see now he had his own Pound too. He screamed at me because he was afraid the painter in him would show." Rayne raised his eyebrows at me and smiled, a beautiful, healing smile of joy. "Monsters may claim creation is weak and, at the same time, create anyway. The difference in the results of their making is a world of destruction or growth. The moment you looked at me, Alex, through your eyes and not Fear's, I remembered my own name. I remembered I love to paint, that truth has always been the same. For years, I painted images of Fear, icy clouds in my own eyes and Pain in yours. I saw only a reflection of broken glass. I pounded and crashed. Desperate to break the fate that 'I was not enough.' I am sorry for how I've made you Fear too. Please keep seeing me. I'd like to fly with you."

I smiled at Rayne and watched his beauty flow. "Of course, I'll always try to see you, though I know my Fear will never fully go."

"We need Fear to keep us alive, but I have a question that will help Us see the trauma through."

"What is it, Rayne?"

"Alex, I'd like to paint your wings before we fly. I see that they're white, but they need something else that's out of your sight."

"I looked at Rayne and offered my hand. His skin felt soft, like a flowing river would. As I touched him, I remembered the powerful flow of running water under my hands. Life. He rushed furiously and passionately through my fingers and up my spine, splashing my wings' roots.

"See now, Alex, look how you're divine."

"What do you mean?"

Rayne spoke softly as he painted, "You created your wings, but I wanted to show you your mind. You think in words and colors, and they weave together more than you might notice."

"It's hard to concentrate on one's own mind, though the mind is the source of all we see."

"I know about clouded vision more than most," Rayne whispered as he painted. "Rage was at my wheel. But let me tell you more about you and how you've made me feel."

"Okay."

"You've seen a rainbow before, yes?"

"Yes, I have many times."

"They're more empowering than most people notice. Your rainbow is what makes you divine."

"I don't understand what you mean," I spoke as Rayne continued to explain while his flowing arms painted.

"The colors of your mind may seem divided, just as a rainbow might. But the colors aren't divided, just distinct. Their distinction is what makes them bright. Each color of you flows long and strong as they mingle with your wings. Each color represents a different strength, right in front of you yet unseen."

"Okay, Rayne, then pick a color. Please tell me what just one means."

"We can tell you as I flow. She's always weaving in between."

We spoke gently as she floated alongside Rayne. We was the breeze behind and in between Rayne's water, peeking with sparkling light-brown eyes as she weaved through him.

"You don't really need to ask about the colors. You can look at Rayne and see for yourself. He is made of water, a reflection. For once, see yourself and not someone else."

My heart relaxed and I looked. I saw red. Bright, angry red at the bottom of my wings, splattered against them as if I were bleeding. Red, a color I had only known as shame. I wanted to see my own reflection, all of me. I expected something beautiful, but shame clouded my eyes. The blood dripped down my wings and onto the floor. The bottom feathers of my wings looked tattered. Bloody and torn.

"I know I am to see beauty, but I can only see what's been shredded."

"It's okay to look at the torn pieces. You don't have to run from blood. To be wounded means you are alive. Bleeding means your heart is beating."

I let myself look at the bottom of my wings. I watched myself bleed. "Rayne, did you paint this blood?"

"No, I am building something else, but you saw blood when you looked at me. When you saw angry red, the color came to be."

"I can create color? Even as you paint?"

"Yes, you can, and it was you who made your wings white."

Well then, I had to ask myself, *why? Was white what I wanted to be?* Purity was associated with the color, but purity wasn't me. Okay, so blood it is then. Shredded, torn, angry. I let myself look, and I felt Rayne paint, but what he was making I couldn't see.

"Just keep looking. Don't be afraid to ask yourself why."

Here I was, thinking I'd see many colors, exactly like the rainbows in books… Red, orange, yellow, green, blue, indigo, and violet, a clear and well-rehearsed pattern. Surely the pattern was what I needed? They would be so harmonious together that I could fly.

"Patterns are what you are breaking. What is known is not always harmony."

Okay then, I thought, *just focus on the red you see now. Keep looking, even as your mind wanders and searches for the familiar.*

Suddenly, I noticed a lamb covered in that same color. Now I know the origins of blood and white. The lamb again was He. I remembered what He told me.

"Separate yourself from the blood. See how you've nailed your shame to The Cross. See how you've slaughtered the creature, slaughtered Him with your very nature. An evil nature."

So I believed I was shredded and torn and that I killed the innocent creature who willingly "died for me."

"No, I didn't!" the angry red cried. "A killer is something I never wanted to be."

But He told me that's what I was, and maybe there's a part of me that wanted to hurt. I won't deny that I am a monster but depraved would never work. My soul is not depraved. I did not slaughter the lamb. Let me look at red again, let me contradict the color's name.

Red can be angry; shredded looks painful. But when I've been angry, I wanted change. I wanted better. Better for my own mind and for the monsters. And what has torn me can teach me how to heal.

"I think you've got something there," We said, and Rayne continued to flow.

As he painted, he asked, "Should I weave the shreds, braid them into something that will grow?"

"No, I don't think so, Rayne. It occurs to me that with the shreds, I can still fly. I would like the color of blood to remind me what We said.

"I don't really want to die."

4

Breathing Blood and Water

I can bleed and I can live; I know how to slow the hurt. As I looked at my wings, the blood cauterized, solidified into a dry but solid foundation. Yes, I'd keep the color; it would protect me from the monsters and myself too.

What other colors can I see? Rayne said something about a rainbow. Nothing is separate. They flow together; I can accept each one as I go. What does color mean together? Where can I find color on my wings? My wings weren't really white if I wanted. What else could there be?

Blue. Finding blue was easy for me. The color of the ocean and skies. I always saw the freedom in blue, but where did it blend with the red?

"Blue crashes like the ocean and spreads like the sky," We said. "Let it crash into your red and stretch into your eyes."

"Waves and sky, of course. That's blue." I looked into Rayne and saw myself and let blue crash as a color too.

Red was stable and dark and, at the same time, bright and maroon. I let blue spill over the top of the red and fill in the foundation of my wings. The blue curled like waves and stretched up my wings to the middle of my spine. Next, I let the blue transform into aqua, mirroring the ocean as it blends blue and green. Then I spun the color up a little higher, so it crashed into the middle of my wings like waves. Rayne smiled as he continued to paint the top, though I still couldn't see which color.

I focused on the aqua I created. Waves were powerful and dangerous, maybe that power could be my mantra.

"Maybe power already was. But not the kind that crucifies. Maybe the power you possess is the same as the skies."

"Power like the skies, what could that mean? The skies shelter and amplify. They remind people of their dreams."

"And there is true power in teaching the world to stretch. The sky is always an example. You can be a blue of hope, an ever shelter untouchable by monsters…and Death."

"There is power in the reminder of power," I told We and Rayne.

Maybe I keep the aqua in my wings and use the color to show others how to fly too. We all are powerful and dangerous, but We can balance that power to serve too.

"What greater gift is there than showing others what they're worth?" Rayne exclaimed. "To paint another in their own eyes is the strongest form I know. If I can help them see for themselves that they are a gift, maybe that joy could grow. Maybe the monster in me will finally willingly go."

"And I suppose then that others don't want to be a monster either, not if someone powerful sees them as something more. But that's where the color gray comes in. I see it knocking at aqua's door."

"Gray"—Rayne stopped painting as he watched the color build like blocks on my wings—"Gray is all I see when I am a monster. Distracted by unresolved wounds."

"I see gray too, Rayne, the color now floods my wings. It builds on red and aqua, and I am reminded of the confusion it brings. Can you tell me what that confusion means to you?"

"I don't know but I can try. Gray is all that I don't understand about myself, and the confusion leads me to avoid wanting to try. Gray is my struggle, the one I cannot name. Gray is the thoughts that race in my head, thoughts that lie and tell me all that exists is blame."

"Who do you blame?"

"Mostly myself. For every hurt I've ever caused. I blame myself for my own misery, mistakes and Should Be swims in them. Gray is so real, though the color itself is bland. I see it stifling red and aqua, gray is all that demands. Gray demands my attention and confuses my past. Gray tells me all the monsters I've ever known are still real. 'Not good enough.' 'Should Be.' 'Failure is shameful.' 'You are failure.' 'You are gray.' 'I DON'T KNOW WHAT YOU ARE SO YOU ARE GRAY!' Gray has no identity. Gray is a muddled reflection of what someone else thought they should be then what they believed I should be. Gray is fractured. Gray is a lie. Gray is why monsters break out and command. Gray captures my mind. Gray is why I cannot see when I am angry. I see only the clouds that shift me into defense. And truth be told, Alex, I don't think gray will go away. I don't think gray will ever stop pushing me to be a monster. And I cannot be confident that I won't give in."

"So what is the answer then? Can We ever escape the monsters?"

"No, but maybe We can learn to live with them."

"Could We create with gray? Could We help the monsters see the color instead of being blinded by it?"

"I think We could. Let's start by keeping gray on your wings. Red, aqua, and gray. Shreds, waves, and blocks. Maybe We can keep building in and with the gray. Maybe I can still paint when I can't see."

And Rayne didn't stop flowing like water, even as his eyes clouded again with gray, threatening a storm. We breezed behind him, not pushing or screaming but making way for Pain.

Rayne looked at Pain and softened. He had been full of Fear as my wings filled with gray. "That reminds me," Rayne whispered, "I no longer want to keep Pain at bay. She has been my enemy and your best friend. I run when she is near. But she has a color and a name too. I will keep painting as she becomes clear."

And Rayne gently brushed my wings while Pain peeked around We's eyes.

"What is your real name then, Pain?" I asked.

"Ardavana," she spoke and didn't scream. Pain's voice was beautiful.

I learned then that she could sing.

Her voice was like a siren, though not one meant to lure. She sang of protection and power and showed me what I could endure.

"Ardavana?" I asked. "What color are you? I ask because I realize your place is around my wings. Instead of hiding, I'd like to fly with you."

"You are right, I can help you fly, and I'd like to stay here, even if I'm not your best friend. Maybe I can be something more. I am the color black, the deep and peaceful night. The reminder that the darkness doesn't have to be where We hide."

"Black is powerful and strong, and the night reminds me of the space we shared. In that space, you were a monster, but you were my protector too. Black is protection. There is shelter in the night."

"Can I blanket your wings as a sheer shield? A veil that covers them when you take flight?"

I saw Ardavana as a beautiful dark veil cascade over my wings, a darkness that showed the colors beneath and floated through the skies. Then I watched as she flowed over me, a flow similar to that of Rayne's. Pain's hair and eyes disintegrated as she beautifully became the skies. She weaved over me and created a veil, and I felt her take root above my wings. Ardavana would always be with me but now as a companion, not as an escape from all the scary things.

1

With the Breath of Night

I was ready to move onto the next color now that I had my veil. I hadn't seen all the colors of my wings, but something drew me back to gray. I realized at this moment that I didn't want the color. Rayne and I recognized that gray was needed, but we didn't really want it. I saw gray as bricks on my wings, something that fit and molded into everything. A solid middle. Needed but not wanted. But I think now that I'd like to want the gray.

Gray reminds me of what I don't understand. And I don't understand many things. Gray has always been a color I wanted to pass through. Move on from my confusion to the end. But I never stop learning how to understand things, and I would like to accept the beauty in learning. Gray was where I believed the monsters reigned, where I believed Pain and Pound had the most power. They existed with their moods, and I didn't understand.

I've always liked words. But one word can change a mood. And it seemed the wrong word could lead to gray. A sentence can bring joy. Or a sentence can summon a monster. Protective instincts govern all when words call defense. So which words are right? Which gray do I want in my sight? What about the other colors? Certainly orange, green, and yellow are warm and living like nature, like the peace I feel in the trees. Gray means a storm. Gray means danger. Gray means I need to take shelter. Gray is cloudy, the same hue I have seen in the monsters' eyes.

"But think for a second. Just one second," said We. "I know your mind is already spinning, but let it wander just a little further. Where are beauty, strength, and most importantly, rightness in the gray?" We shimmered as she spoke and floated; her beautiful brown eyes glowing peace.

I looked at We a moment then closed my eyes and breathed.

2

I will start with the last word she said, "rightness." Now that is a word that shifts all. What is the balance between right and wrong in morality? How do we abandon the ego-driven "need" to be right? I don't always have to be right, though the monsters in me say I do. A burning desire to be correct has distracted me from what I could learn in the gray.

Sometimes people have to be right. Without right, there can be no justice. But what have I missed rushing through gray, determined that I was right if black or white? I mean arguments. I mean lack of empathy. I mean seeing only through my own eyes. I mean running from gray because I believed I needed to be right to survive.

But I don't. I really don't. There's also that option. Let me look at the other two words. Beauty. Strength. Beauty and strength in gray. The strength and stretch of listening to another, all empathy has happened in gray. I feel the most at peace when I listen, when I am reasoning and keeping selfishness at bay. Words can shift a mood. Maybe that's not always bad. I am going to happily keep gray in my wings, building blocks of bricks.

Gray is where beauty rests. Nothing is more gorgeous than gray. The humility of gray means humans are willing to learn, and they take their monsters with them too. I am looking up in my room now, realizing I haven't described it yet to you.

I write in the dark, but really the dark is gray. My shades are drawn and the shadows are long. My pencil edge sweeps gracefully gray words across the page. Words of the monsters, words of me, and words of We that I have shared with you. I write in the gray, keeping the comfort of my wooden stool and desk near. In this gray place, I have seen the monsters, and I have allowed them to look at you. Even now, Pound is still here, reading over my shoulder.

"I see myself in your words," he whispered. "And I whispered to you of the new name I desired." Pound whispered to me with his bloodshot lips, sometimes I still smell whiskey in his breath. But he flows like Rayne beside me too, still painting my wings as I write.

"Rayne, I remembered that I still don't know… What color are you painting? What are you making on the top of my wings?"

"Something you've seen before, though I hope I can help you see more… I…" His voice begins to fade, though he is whispering close to my ear.

I realize then, it's Pain again, screaming on my back. Pain is still here too, and I recall how her blond hair shimmered in the sun. For a moment, I feel her veil as a heavy weight, a load on my back instead of a protective veil.

"It's okay, Pain. You have a new name. Remember that you are Ardavana. You can still protect me without screaming. I'll feel you every time I brush up against danger."

"But who then is your best friend?" Pain's scream was veiled but clear.

We is near and she's made things clear… We can't worry about who will take which space. My best friend is my own mind, and We are together, the best way to face this world is together. I am We and so are you. Though We will always be monsters too.

3

I was writing in the gray, but the sun had gone down. The room was blanketed in darkness. I had always feared darkness. I didn't like what might creep around me in the night. Which eyes might peer in the shadows? Usually Pain's smiling ones.

As Ardavana spoke with me, I heard Rayne raise his voice, "Look out into the darkness, but only if you choose…"

I raised my head, absolutely terrified knowing a dark space lurked before me. I stared in that space, an empty room, and heard myself say, *They can't hurt you.* I had always whispered in the darkness, afraid to wake the voices in the night if I was too loud. As I stared into that space, I saw what I could create. Rayne was before me, flowing like water, then he flowed into Pound. Clean-cut Pound with bursting red blood vessels in his nose and lips, Pain screaming as she materialized beside him and faded into Ardavana as she covered me with her veil, pinned near the roots of my wings. Then Rayne held up a mirror, so I could see all that was in between. The mirror showed me the top of my wings, stretching up above my head, and in that space, I finally understood grace, the top of my wings another reflection.

Rayne had painted a mirror on top of both my wings. The reflection stretched high. My wings shimmered with beauty as the mirror flowed, similar to Rayne's water.

"A reflection is the point," Rayne whispered as his water rushed through me, healing my skin and my eyes.

Then all the monsters spoke through me, their deep voices as one slipping off my lips. Rayne, Ardavana, Pain, Pound, Alex—Me. We were We.

I looked at my face in the mirror and watched my mouth move gracefully as We spoke, "You are the creator. The monsters are real because they were in your mind and across the earth. All monsters are real because they are human creations. You are a creation. But deconstruct what truth means to you. Pound was a threat. Pain was a threat. They were outside you and they were real. Then your mind flexed her strength and became We, flying over Death as he reached for the wheel. Remember when We was a ghost in your hand? She is divine as are you. Look at your face, accept our embrace, and know that we became monsters to keep you safe."

The darkness didn't really make sense. I began to feel incoherent and insane. But my mind was always spinning. Humans have the power to create all the time no matter the damage that has been done. The monsters asked me to see We beside them, to understand that I had always won.

There was a Pound of whiskey who scratched my heart; the illogical nature of his attacks felt like shards of glass. But I picked up the pieces and created Pain, aware that the bleeding wouldn't last. My body created Pain to keep me safe. And I accepted her as my best friend. Pound knocked on my door and reminded me I wanted more; my heart beat heavy as I cringed at his bloodshot face. My heart was real and full of guilt. He always made me feel like I was wrong. But in the darkness and in the danger, I learned guilt and shame weren't where I belonged.

I sought darkness and danger and reflected on them in the gray. We painted wings of beautiful things, and I forever desire to see myself this way. I looked at Our eyes in the mirror, full of someone who'd "been through it." Then I thought of other dark places that I feared, a crawl space at the base of the house, near the room where I wrote. It's not a place of fear or a place of ghosts but rather a foundation. In dark places, there is space to breathe; I don't have to sit in the light of what others perceive. And perceptions are everything, for me and all the monsters. I am not alone in this world. Humans are everything, and they can build everything. I see I am divine; I have wings that I have weaved that surpass time. I can use them to fly to others. I see in the mirror that the monsters will always be near, and I can choose to run or fly.

"I don't understand," Ardavana said as her veil covered me.

"I just mean I am going to stop running. I have seen real monsters, and I have believed they pounded on my door when my heart was afraid. The monsters won't ever go away. I have seen you, Pain, Ardavana, still smiling in the dark as I write, still waiting to scream and hold me tight. And I know that if Pound scares me enough, I might let you. The difference now is that I know your names. You are a protector, and Pound is a warning. Rayne is a creator and We is me, Alex. We is the voice that has shown me that I am more than monsters, even when I became one as I ran from them."

"So what about the world then?" Ardavana spoke. "What do people make if they are not monsters?"

"I think the point is that We are monsters, but We are many other shades too. And We can't be afraid to look at ourselves… Rayne, Ardavana, Pound, Pain…all exist at once. Use the mirror Rayne painted to look at our wings. They reflect the creation of the world. A base of blood, a curling wave of blue, broad, gray bricks and a mirror too. Blood flows and gives life, water flows and restores, gray builds and learns. And mirrors remind us to always look at ourselves, not just in moments of vanity but in truth too. We need to see who We are with the monsters. The lies and the running were where I lost you."

We looked into our eyes and saw the skies, the brightness of where We could stretch. Then We stretched our wings and thought of beautiful things, increasing our awareness of what the mind could bring. What beautiful things do people make? And what makes us divine? Blood, water, building, reflection, and the ability to understand our own minds.

"I am anxious, I think. We spoke together. Anxious to protect and anxious to create. And We have created much during this time of fear. People make beauty. People see each other. They weave themselves together through an invisible thread. They create in mud million-dollar homes, rivers, kitchens, and words. Shelters, music, filtration, and the unknown. Most importantly, the unknown."

"I understand," Ardavana said. "So I think I'd like to see Us without shame. I would like to believe in what We can do. We are not depraved destroyers, though We may see ourselves as more powerful when we construct that way sometimes." She wrapped her arms around me and, for once, Ardavana and I fell into a dream, not a nightmare.

We held each other close on our way into the night…

We flew through space with our wings. Ardavana wrapped me in her veil as we floated up, up, and up until we broke through the layers of the earth into the dark sky, sprinkled with stars. Our wings carried Us, and Ardavana protected Us. Mirror, gray, waves, and blood. We floated and soared until we approached a star. The creature burned with desire. Furiously beautiful orange flames circled a gray, shadowy mass.

The shadow pulsed with life then spoke deeply with a woman's voice, "I am Iron, crafted to bring air to the blood in your wings and body. I am the core of the earth."

Alongside Iron floated Hydrogen. The same shadowy mass and flames but with a smooth, light female voice. She spoke gently, "I am Hydrogen, the first. I flow in your wings as water and hydrate the earth with my waves."

"I can speak too." Another mass floated near Ardavana and I. She took deep, intentional breaths as her voice rose up like a melody, "I am Oxygen. I give life to the air you fly inside and breathe. I smile with your counts of four."

Breath. I remember her. She is always in my lungs and wings, yet I often forget how to help her move.

"Breathe, Ardavana," We whispered.

Oxygen's flames grew stronger and wider as Ardavana and I breathed together.

"One, two, three, four," We sang with Oxygen and floated higher.

A fourth star greeted us as we breathed. His voice was deep and comforting as he spoke, "Carbon. I am your spine and the branches of your wings. I've held you up even when you believed you had fallen."

We felt strength as Carbon spoke. We took a moment to feel muscles that held our spine and wings. We were strength. We are.

A final star appeared alongside Carbon, and the five of them formed into a circle, each burning into the other. "Nitrogen," he whispered, but the whisper was strong, foundational, and fluid. "I am the energy that connects all life, the invisible thread you sense but cannot see. Though I am confident you see me now."

"We do," We all spoke. Then We lit up with orange flames, just like the stars.

The flames circled my wings in a protective fire. The beauty of the stardust floated and clung to us. The stars had been our wings and circled our wings.

"Remember where you come from when you believe you are only a monster. Remember that you are stardust. Remember that you can create as we do. You have. You are a being of the heavens and stars, crafted to shelter the earth."

We all smiled. We found joy. We flew with a new strength in our wings through space. We loved the stars, but We belonged on earth. We needed to remind the world that they were crafted from the stars, monstrous and gentle. We had a mission to spread the peace that had flooded our bodies. Peace, creation, and protection—the shelter of a family. Our family was the earth, ocean, and each other.

We flew down, back into earth powerfully and confidently. As We reached earth, We saw and smelled the ocean in the night, scents of salt and clarity. She rushed. She sang. Her waves climbed and roared and rang with joy, protecting all of the life inside her. We sat with her on the shore. Our flames glowed in the darkness, and the ocean painted our feet. We gripped the sand in joy, rooting ourselves to the earth, watching the ocean crash over our skin and pull our rage away. The ocean was big and powerful. She could carry and dissolve the weight of our trauma, the fear that created monsters. And We promised We would take care of her too. We promised to spread stardust across the land. We promised to use the will of monsters to protect and warn, rather than destroy. Under the sky and wrapped in the ocean, We learned that we could switch on protective instincts if we needed them; we didn't have to live inside them. Ardavana knew how to protect; she would be a veil across the earth. Rayne would paint an earth in balance. An earth that knew how to grow. We would take care of the shores that the ocean held. Ocean, sand, and hands. Creators.

"Bang! Bang! Bang! Silence. Bang!"

I shook my head from side to side and dropped my pencil. My vision of the ocean dissolved, and I saw the gray room before me. Someone was banging on the door of my room. They want to get inside. They don't want to talk. They want to destroy.

Death. Here.

"We have to open the door," Rayne, Pain, Pound, Ardavana, and I spoke quickly. "We have to open the door, or She will break in. Shedeath. We know She's here. We've been waiting, ever since Pound's warning in the night."

Pound's warning reminded me who Shedeath is.

"This monstrous Death is not the creature who welcomes you the moment you die," he said steadily. "Shedeath is everything that drains your life while you live. Shedeath feeds on all your joy, willpower, intentions, and energy."

I knew Pound was right. When Shedeath is near, I am on fire. My instincts are on fire. I can't see. I can't hear. I only burn.

I braced myself and saw that I still had my wings. They glowed with stardust, cloaked with the veil of Ardavana's protection. We opened the door, and She was there. Death wasn't He this time. It was indeed She. Shedeath. I remembered Her face and Her hair. White. Blond. Blue eyes of rage, just like the other Death. Cold. Empty. She instantly lunged as I opened the door but not for my throat like the other Death. She lunged at my wings. Shedeath looked like Pain, but She was certainly not a friend. Shedeath wasn't in the mirror, and She wasn't in my mind. Shedeath was a true monster. Dead yet feasting on the living.

"I will rip you apart!" She hissed and tore at my wings. Her hiss slithered like a scream.

"Why are you angry! What do you want here?!" I made an *X* with my arms as I blocked Her from clawing at my wings and face.

Her white bony limbs flew and twisted in a wild rage. She clawed, punched, and ripped at my skin, desperate to shred and mutilate my wings.

Her hiss echoed into a terrible scream, "I WANT ME! You stole everything from me! This is all your fault! FUCK YOU! FUCK YOU! FUCK YOU! I HATE YOU! I HATE YOU! I HATE YOU! And I'll never stop! The world doesn't see me! The world circles you! The stars breathe into YOU! I HAD EVERYTHING! I SHOULD HAVE EVERYTHING!" Shedeath's terrible scream echoed louder as She tried to punch at the mirror in my wings, Her wild fists desperately seeking to shatter the glass.

I braced Us, terrified. "You need to leave," I said matter-of-factly. I knew I couldn't hit Her back.

Shedeath was a monster who I would never overcome with violence. Nothing is ever won with violence. Not really.

"I am not leaving without your pencil and your wings!" Her voice pierced the air, high and shrill. "You will listen to me! You will hear me! You will do everything I want! You owe me! You owe me! You owe me!

"What do I owe you for?" We asked as Shedeath warped into a tornado of fists and claws.

"You know what for! You need to fix it! You need to change! I am going to count, too, but I will count backwards so you know it's a threat. So you know I am coming! Give me...me back! Nooooooowwww! Four...three...two...one."

...

Shedeath's fury boiled out of control as She stopped clawing at my wings and lunged for my pencil, my creator, and the control I had of my own mind. Shedeath almost knocked me over, rushing past me as She lunged for sanity, though She didn't really want sanity. Shedeath only wants to destroy and mutilate. I knew then that Shedeath was going to stab me with my pencil since She failed to shred my wings. I sensed Her intentions with an alertness that went beyond sight, beyond noise. Suddenly, I was grateful for all the monsters before Her and what they had taught me. I knew how to fight. Most importantly, I learned that my pencil, creation, and mastery of my own mind was every piece of the world worth protecting. I would fight for my life. I would fight Her for everything. As I began to stumble, I remembered that I had wings. The blood on the bottom created a hard crust that caught me. I found my balance. Shedeath didn't know I had been fighting monsters my whole life. In my reflection, She saw a face that appeared to be whole, unmarred by monsters. My wings tipped me back up, and I turned toward Her as She snatched my pencil. I pried Shedeath's fingers off as She gripped desperately. I remember Her fingers. White, bony claws. The grip and hands of a monster. The choke hold of all my nightmares.

She stared into me with empty eyes, the eyes of a monster who knew nothing beyond Herself. The eyes of a mind that knew nothing of wings except that She wanted to destroy them because they didn't belong to Her. My eyes burned amber with stardust back into Shedeath's as I gathered all the power in my wings… Mirror—the power to see myself as a monster, human, and creator to know how my intentions could influence others for better or worse. Gray—all the strength I held even when I didn't understand, the power to learn. Shedeath didn't learn. Just destroyed. Blood—the life in my wings and inside me that makes all my muscles move, the blood that remained inside me while past monsters tried to destroy. And water—waves like the ocean's peace, power, and comfort; hydration, a life force, a graceful power that Shedeath would never understand.

We glowed with stardust. Our body blazed with fire and surrounded the mirror on Our wings. For a brief moment, the monster saw Herself in the mirror. Shedeath screeched with fury as She stared back into Her own empty eyes. She couldn't see herself as a monster. She only saw empty. She saw nothing, and the empty reflection terrified Her. Shedeath can only see Herself in others, penetrating their life force like a parasite. Shedeath feared the mirror because She would never find the glory She grasped at.

Just as Shedeath reached for the mirror on Our wings, every ounce of Her intending to shatter the glass, She burned Her fingers on the heat of stardust. Shedeath couldn't stand the fire. She squealed as She saw Herself empty in the mirror of our wings and looked at Her scorched hands. The heat burned Her away. We watched Shedeath slowly disintegrate with the light of stars with the knowledge that She had no power in a world that was not created for Her alone.

True monsters always self-destruct.

One

The world was created for We. For Us. For everyone to create, share, and protect. Shedeath couldn't reign on earth or in the stars. I watched every piece of Her dissolve and disintegrate into the air, like dust. Out-of-date and unseen. She melted into Her own reflection, an empty abyss. She couldn't win in a world of stardust. Reflections were never meant to last. Really, Shedeath was as fragile and empty as Her face appeared in the mirror. Her remains slowly faded as the sun set outside Our room.

Shedeath was gone. My pencil remained. My wings glowed. We were whole. And We knew what We needed to do. Monsters are created when people believe that they are not enough. A monster like Shedeath was created when She was taught that She was everything. We needed to create a world of balance, a world where people see who they are and what they have to learn. Most importantly, they see each other. A world where people know that they are monsters, but they can create something more. Our monsters are how we survive, not how we exist.

Rayne said, "I can help you paint with your pencil. I can paint the sky alongside you. Fill the earth with your pencil."

"Absolutely, Rayne, we'll paint together."

Rayne smiled as his arms flowed like a river, and he grabbed his brush. We remained in the gray room. We didn't need to wait until morning to see the sky. We remembered its blue hue. I picked up my pencil. The navy wood began to shine with stardust as I lifted her above Shedeath's remains. The space where Shedeath left Her rage became orange and bright. Orange, the color of sunset, the color of the sunset in the ocean.

"Rayne, let's make a world of sunset. Beautiful orange that reminds us that we can be confident and safe, even as night approaches. Orange, the color of stardust."

"Okay," Rayne responded gently. "How do we show the world that they are made of stardust?"

"We remind them that stars burn. Pain burns. Burning means we're alive, but we don't have to spread fire."

Rayne cringed a moment as he remembered himself as Pound. A frown materialized and the river of his body rippled.

"It's okay, Rayne. Don't live in shame. We have all been Pound. But Pound is not who you are. He is how you defend yourself, and the deadly monsters of the world remind us that we should be afraid."

"So where do I keep Pound then?" He paused and stared at his brush.

"In your heart, beating safely and steadily. Tell him that it's okay for him to beat steadily. He doesn't have to come out unless a real monster comes, like Shedeath."

"And I am wise enough to learn the difference between monsters and safety?"

We smiled at Rayne. "Yes, you are."

A quiet pause rose in the air, and I remembered Shedeath. I shuddered at the memory of Her pale blue eyes frozen in fury. I recalled Her claws as they tore at me, goblin-like and reeking of the death She carried. For a moment, my heart pounded. Shedeath fully materialized in my mind, white, blond hair blowing wildly. She felt real again.

"It's okay," Ardavana whispered as she cloaked my back. "I have learned how to be a friend. Shedeath caused you pain, and it's okay to feel the scars She left. But We will protect you if you are in true danger. And you are not in danger now. You are safe in the space you made, here in the gray. Let's write a picture for others to see that safety too."

"Write about the flower," Rayne said. "Write about your wings."

We remembered the buzz in my skin as I rested under the sun and breathed deeply while We whispered. Safe is the human ability to calm their body and build shelters. Remember how to look at the flower, to stare at the purple hues until they nestle near your heart. Focus on their brightness, not what lurks over your shoulder, deep in the past. The earth shelters its humans and calms them with the breath of all things that grow. We remember the sun that rested on our skin, reminding us that we can be warm when we're lonely. Our skin answers to the sun; our pores remember stardust, where we first burned into existence. We created the earth, and We are the earth. Safety means looking up to the sky and feeling the heat, not restlessly over our shoulders. Not into the past in shame. We learn from the past. We don't avoid it, but We also do not burn in shame. We accept our Pain as a friend and show her how to learn to protect without stinging. We remind Pound that he doesn't have to bang like Death. He can knock steadily. He can remember that doors are open. He is a painter; he is a creator. A safe world is one where people remember that they belong. We can grow to understand each flower's color, each tree's whisper, and the gifts that each human can create, that our heartbeats can synchronize. A safe world is one where we don't compare. Death, the monster, needed to feel above to survive. We are not above. We are not survival alone. We can switch on survival when We need to. We are each other, and We are ourselves. We become our best selves when we shelter the earth and accept her protection in return. We are born of stardust, the supernatural. All life is supernatural. We will live inside what we can't explain.

I kissed my pencil, navy like the sky and glowing with stardust. What a gift my pencil has been. My pencil showed me my mind; she showed me We and the gift of creation that makes this world burn bright. Monsters are real. We can run with them.

About the Author

Jenna Dill is an author and high school English teacher from the Midwest. Every day, she is inspired by the beauty of words and how they have the power to shape, build, and add value to human life. Her passion for teaching and learning is the same passion that drives her motivation to write. With the success of *Sheltered*, her debut novel, she continues to explore the literary world in multiple genres. Her dream is to empower others with her words and continue to live a life of love, personal growth, and creativity. One of her favorite authors is Trevor Noah, who stated, "Love is a creative act. When you love someone, you create a new world for them." She hopes that readers will find the courage to love themselves creatively, to look back on past monsters and regrets and see how the dark times carried them to the present and onto a future of hope. As Jenna's character, Sarah, learned in her novel, *Sheltered*, "We can find pieces of ourselves in dark places. Many fear who they will become in the darkness or what might consume them inside it. But darkness can also help us find the freedom to understand the pieces of ourselves that we can't see–that even others can't see. In every dark piece, there's a purpose. Collect the piece you need there and allow it to take shape in the light."

Printed in the USA
CPSIA information can be obtained
at www.ICGtesting.com
LVHW090751090524
779700LV00002B/264